CONSIGNMENT

Start Publishing PD LLC

Manufactured in the United States of America

Cover art: Shutterstock/Taisiya Kozorez

Cover design: Jennifer Do

10 9 8 7 6 5 4 3 2 1

ISBN 979-8-8809-0339-9

CONSIGNMENT

by Alan E. Nourse

The three shots ripped through the close night air of the prison, sharply, unbelievably. Three guards crumpled like puppets in the dead silence that followed. The thought flashed through Krenner's mind, incredibly, that possibly no one had heard.

He hurled the rope with all his might up the towering rock wall, waited a long eternity as the slim strong line swished through the darkness, and heard the dull "clank" as the hook took hold at the top. Like a cat he started up, frantically, scrambling, and climbing, the sharp heat of the rope searing his fingers. Suddenly daylight was around him, the bright unearthly glare of arc lights, the siren cutting in with its fierce scream. The shouts of alarm were far below him as he fought up the line, knot after knot, the carefully prepared knots. Twenty seconds to climb, he thought, just twenty seconds—

*

Rifle shots rang out below, the shells smashing into the concrete around him. Krenner almost turned and snarled at the little circle of men in the glaring light below, but turning meant precious seconds. A dull, painful blow struck his foot, as his hands grasped the jagged glass at the top of the wall.

In a moment of triumph he crouched at the top and laughed at the little men and the blazing guns below; on the other side lay the blackness of the river. He turned and plunged into the blackness, his foot throbbing, down swiftly until the cool wetness of the river closed about him, soothing his pain, bathing his mind in the terrible beauty of freedom, and what went with freedom. A few dozen powerful strokes would carry him across and down the river, three miles below the prison fortress from which he had broken. Across the hill from that, somewhere, he'd find Sherman and a wide open road to freedom—

*

CONSIGNMENT

Free! Twenty-seven years of walls and work, bitterness and hateful, growing, simmering revenge. Twenty-seven years for a fast-moving world to leave him behind, far behind. He'd have to be careful about that. He wouldn't know about things. Twenty-seven years from his life, to kill his ambition, to take his woman, to disgrace him in the eyes of society. But the candle had burned through. He was free, with time, free, easy, patient time, to find Markson, search him out, kill him at last.

Hours passed it seemed, in the cold, moving water. Krenner struggled to stay alert; loss of control now would be sure death. A few shots had followed him from the wall behind, hopeless shots, hopeless little spears of light cutting across the water, searching for him, a tiny dot in the blackness. Radar could never spot him, for he wore no metal, and the sound of his movements in the water were covered by the sighing wind and the splashing of water against the prison walls.

Finally, after ages of pain and coldness, he dragged himself out onto the muddy shore, close to the calculated spot. He sat on the edge and panted, his foot swollen and throbbing. He wanted to scream in pain, but screams would bring farmers and dogs and questions. That would not do, until he found Sherman, somewhere back in those hills, with a 'copter, and food, and medication, and quiet, peaceful rest.

He tried to struggle to his feet, but the pain was too much now. He half walked, half dragged himself into the woods, and started as best he could the trek across the hills.

*

Jerome Markson absently snapped on the radiovisor on his desk. Sipping his morning coffee thoughtfully as he leafed through the reports on his desk, he listened with half an ear until the announcer's voice seeped through to his consciousness. He tightened suddenly in his seat, and the coffee cooled before him, forgotten.

"—Eastern Pennsylvania is broadcasting a four-state alarm with special radiovisor pictures in an effort to pick up the trail of a convict who escaped the Federal Prison here last night. The escaped man, who shot and killed two guards making good his escape, dived into the river adjoining the prison, and is believed to have headed for an outside rendezvous somewhere in the Blue Mountain region. The prisoner is John Krenner, age 51, gray hair, blue eyes, five-foot-nine. He is armed and dangerous, with four unsuccessful escape attempts, and three known murders on his record. He was serving a life term, without leniency, for the brutal murder in July, 1967, of Florence Markson, wife of the now-famous industrialist, Jerome Markson, president of Markson Foundries. Any person with information of this man's whereabouts should report—"

Markson stared unbelieving at the face which appeared in the visor. Krenner, all right. The same cold eyes, the same cruel mouth, the same sneer. He snapped off the set, his face white and drawn. To face the bitter, unreasoning hate of this man, his former partner—even a prison couldn't hold him.

A telephone buzzed, shattering the silence of the huge office.

"Hello, Jerry? This is Floyd Gunn in Pittsburgh. Krenner's escaped!"

"I know. I just heard. Any word?"

"None yet. We got some inside dope from one of the men in the prison that he has an outside escape route, and that he's been digging up all the information he could find in the past three months or so about the Roads. But I wanted to warn you." The policeman's voice sounded distant and unreal. "He promised to get you, Jerry. I'm ordering you and your home heavily guarded—"

"Guards won't do any good," said Markson, heavily. "Krenner will get me if you don't get him first. Do everything you can."

The policeman's voice sounded more cheerful. "At any rate, he's in the eastern part of the state now. He has four hundred miles to travel before he can get to you. Unless he has a 'copter, or somehow gets on the Roads, he can't get to you for a day or so. We're doing everything we can."

Markson hung up the receiver heavily. Twenty-seven years of peace since that devil had finally murdered his way out of his life. And now he was back again. A terrible mistake for a partner, a man with no reason, a man who could not understand the difference between right and wrong. A man with ruthless ambition, who turned on his partner when honesty got in his way, and murdered his partner's wife in rage when his own way of business was blocked. A man so twisted with rage that he threatened on the brink of capital punishment to tear Markson's heart out, yet Markson had saved him from the chair. An appeal, some money, some influence, had snatched him from death's sure grasp, so he could come back to kill again. And a man with such diabolical good fortune that he could now come safely to Markson, and hunt him out, and carry out the fancied revenge that his twisted mind demanded.

Markson took the visiphone in hand again and dialed a number. The face of a young girl appeared. "Hi, dad. Did you see the news report?"

"Yes, I saw it. I want you to round up Jerry and Mike and take the 'copter out to the summer place on Nantucket. Wait for me there. I don't know how soon I can make it, but I don't want you here now. Leave immediately."

The girl knew better than to argue with her father. "Dad, is there any chance—?"

"There's lots of chance. That's why I want you away from here."

He flipped off the connection, and sighed apprehensively. Now to wait. The furnaces had to keep going, the steel had to be turned out, one way or another. He'd have to stay. And hope. Perhaps the police *would* get him—

*

The elderly lady sat on the edge of the kitchen chair, shivering. "We'll be glad to help you, but you won't hurt us, will you?"

"Shut up," said Krenner. The gray plastic of his pistol gleamed dully in the poor light of the farm kitchen. "Get that foot dressed, with tight pressure and plenty of 'mycin. I don't want it to bleed, and I don't want an infection." The woman hurried her movements, swiftly wrapping the swollen foot.

The man lifted a sizzling frying pan from the range, flipping a hamburger onto a plate. He added potatoes and carrots. "Here's the food," he said sullenly. "And you might put the gun away. We don't have weapons, and we don't have a 'phone."

"You have legs," snapped Krenner. "Now shut up."

The woman finished the dressing. "Try it," she said. The convict stood up by the chair, placing his weight on the foot gingerly. Pain leaped through his leg, but it was a clean pain. He could stand it. He took a small map from his pocket. "Any streams or gorges overland between here and Garret Valley?"

The farmer, shook, his head. "No."

"Give me some clothes, then. No, don't leave. The ones you have on."

The farmer slipped out of his clothes silently, and Krenner dropped the prison grays in the corner.

"You'll keep your mouths shut about this," he stated flatly.

"Oh, yes, you can count on us," exclaimed the woman, eyeing the gun fearfully. "We won't tell a soul."

"I'll say you won't," said Krenner, his fingers tightening on the gun. The shots were muted and flat in the stillness of the kitchen.

An hour later Krenner broke through the underbrush, crossed a rutted road, and pushed on over the ridge. His cruel face was dripping with perspiration. "It should be the last ridge," he thought. "I've gone a good, three miles—" The morning sun was bright, filtering down through the trees, making beautiful wet patterns on the damp ground. The morning heat was just beginning, but the food and medications had made progress easy. He pulled himself up onto a rock ledge, over to the edge, and felt his heart stop cold as he peered down into the valley below.

A dark blue police 'copter nestled on the valley floor next to the sleek gray one. It must have just arrived, for the dark uniforms of the police were swarming around the gray machine He saw the pink face and the sporty clothes of the occupant as he came down the ladder, his hands in the air.

Too late! They'd caught Sherman!

He lay back shaking.

Impossible! He *had* to have Sherman. They couldn't possibly have known, unless somehow they had foreseen, or heard—. His mind seethed with helpless rage. Without Sherman he was stuck. No way to reach Markson, no way to settle that score—unless possibly—.

The Roads.

He'd heard about them. Way back in 1967 when he'd gone up, the roads were underway. A whole system of Rolling Roads was proposed then, and the first had already been built, between Pittsburgh and the Lakes. A crude affair, a conveyor belt system, running at a steady seventy-five miles per hour, carrying only ore and freight.

But in the passing years reports had filtered through the prison walls. New men, coming "up for a visit" had brought tales, gross exaggerations, of the Rolling Roads grown huge, a tremendous system building itself up, crossing hills and valleys in unbroken lines, closed in from weather and hijackers, fast and smooth and endless. Criss-crossing the nation, they had said, in never-slowing belts of passengers and freight livestock. The Great Triangle had been first, from Chicago to St. Louis to Old New York, and back to Chicago. Now every town, every village had its small branch, its entrance to the Rolling Roads, and once a man got on the Roads, they had said, he was safe until he tried to get off.

Clearly the memory of the reports filtered through Krenner's mind. The great Central Roads run from Old New York to Chicago, through New Washington and Pittsburgh—

Markson was in Pittsburgh—

Krenner started down through the underbrush, travelling south by the sun, the urgency of his mission spurring him on against the pain of his foot, the difficulty of the terrain over which he travelled. He was too far north. Somewhere to the south he'd find the Roads. And once on the Roads, he'd find a way to get off—

*

He stopped at the brink of the hill and gasped in amazement.

They ran across the wide valley like silver ribbons. The late afternoon sunlight reflected gold and pink from the plasti-glass encasement, concealing the rushing line of travel within the covering. Like twin serpents, they lay across the hills, about a mile apart, the Road travelling east, and the Road moving west. They stretched as far as he could see. And he could see the white sign which said, "Merryvale Entrance, Westbound, Three miles."

As he tramped, across the field he could hear the hum of the Roads grow loud in his ears. An automatic, machinelike hum, a rhythm of motion. Close to the westbound road he moved back eastward along it, toward the little port which formed the entrance to it. And soon he saw the police 'copter which rested near the entrance, and the uniformed men with their rifles, alert. Three of them.

Krenner fingered his weapon easily. It was almost dark; they would not see him easily. He kept a small hill between himself and the police and moved in within gunshot range. He could see the rocket-like car resting on its single rail, waiting for a passenger to enter, to touch the button which would activate the tiny rocket engines and move it forward, ever and ever more swiftly until it reached the acceleration of the Roads, and slid over, and became a part of the Road. Moving carefully, he slipped from rock to rock, closer to the car and the men who guarded it.

Suddenly the bay of a hound cut through the gloom. Two small brown dogs with the men, straining at their leashes. He hadn't counted on that. Swiftly he took cover and lined his sights with the blue uniforms. Before they knew even his approximate location he had cut them down, and the dogs also, and raced wildly down the remainder of the hill to the car.

"Fare may be calculated from the accompanying charts, and will be collected when your car has taken its place on the Roads," said a little sign near the cockpit. Krenner studied the dashboard for a moment, then jammed in the button marked "Forward," and settled back. The monorail slid forward without a sound, and plunged into a tunnel in the hill. Out the other side, with ever-increasing acceleration it slid in alongside the gleaming silver ribbon, faster and faster. With growing apprehension Krenner watched the speedometer mount, past two hundred, two hundred and twenty, forty, sixty, eighty—at three hundred miles per hour the acceleration force eased, and the car suddenly swerved to the left, into a dark causeway. And then into the brightly lighted plasti-glass tunnel.

He was on the Roads!

Alongside the outside lane the little car sped, moving on an independent rail, sliding gently past other cars resting on the middle lane. An opening appeared, and Krenner's car slid over another notch, disengaged its rail, and settled to a stop on the central lane of the Road. The speedometer fell to nothing, for the car's motion was no longer independent, but an integral part of the speeding Road itself. Three hundred miles per hour on a constant, nonstop flight across the rolling land.

A loudspeaker suddenly piped up in his car. "Welcome to the Roads," it said. "Your fare collector will be with you in a short while. After he has arrived, feel free to leave your car and be at ease on the Road outside. Eating, resting, and sleeping quarters will be found at regular intervals. You are warned, however, not to cross either the barriers to the outside lanes, nor the barriers to the freight-carrying areas front and rear. Pleasant travelling."

Krenner chuckled grimly, and settled down in his car, his automatic in his hand. His fare collector would get a surprise. Down the Road a short distance he saw the man approaching, wearing the green uniform of the Roads. And then he stiffened. Three blue uniforms were accompanying him. Opening the car door swiftly, he slipped out onto the soft carpeting of the Road, and raced swiftly away from the approaching men.

They saw him when he started to run. Ahead he could see a crowd of passengers around a dining area. A shout went up as he knocked a woman down in his pell-mell flight, but he was beyond them in an instant. His foot hindered him, and his pursuers were gaining. Suddenly before him he saw a barrier—a four foot metal wall. No carpet beyond it, no furnishings along the sides. A freight area! He hopped over the barrier and plunged into the blackness of the freight tunnel as he heard the shouts of his pursuers. "Stop! Come back! Stop or we'll shoot!"

They didn't shoot. In a moment Krenner came to the first freight carrier, one of the standard metal containers resting on the steel of the Road. He ran past it, and the next. The third and fourth were open cars, stacked high with machinery. He ran on for several moments before he glanced back.

They weren't following him any more. He could see them, far back, where the light began, a whole crowd of people at the barrier he had crossed. But no one followed him. Odd that they should stop. He centered his mind more closely on his surroundings. Freight might conceal him to get him off the Roads where no passenger station would ever let him through. He climbed to the top of a nearby freight container and slipped down in. Chunks of rock were under his feet, and he fell in a heap on the hard bed. What possible kind of freight—? He slipped a lighter from his pocket and snapped it on.

Coal! A normal freight load. He climbed back up and looked along the road. No pursuit. An uneasy chill went through him—this was too easy. To ride a coal car to safety, without a single man pursuing him—to where? He examined the billing on the side of the car, and he forgot his fears in the rush of excitement. The billing read, "Consignment: Coal, twenty tons, Markson Foundries, via Pittsburgh private cutoff."

His car was carrying him to Markson!

His mind was full of the old, ugly hate, the fearful joy of the impending revenge. Fortune's boy, he thought to himself. Even Sherman could not have done so well, to ride the Rolling Roads, not just to Pittsburgh, not to the mountains, but right to Markson's backyard! He shivered with anticipation. Pittsburgh was only a few hundred miles away, and at three hundred miles an hour—Krenner clenched his fists in cruel pleasure. He hadn't long to wait.

*

An hour passed slowly. Krenner's leg was growing stiff after the exertion of running. Still no sign of life. He eased his position, and stiffened when he heard the little relay box above the consignment sheet give a couple of sharp clicks.

Near the end! He hugged himself in excitement. What a neat trick, to ride a consignment of coal to the very yards where Markson would be! The coal yards which he might have owned, the furnaces, the foundry—. There would be men there to receive the car from the line, well he could remember the men, day and night, working and sweating in those yards and mills! There would be men there to brake the car and empty it. He was in old clothes, farm clothes—he would fit in so well; as soon as the car slowed he could jump off, and simply join the other men. Or he could shoot, if he had to. A little agility in getting out of the car, and a little care in inquiring the way to Markson's office—

The car suddenly shifted to the outer lane. Krenner gripped a handle on the inside and held tight. He felt the swerving motion, and suddenly the car moved out of the tunnel into the open night air. He climbed up the side and peered over the edge. There were five cars in the consignment; he was on the last. Travelling almost at Road speed along the auxiliary cutoff. Swiftly they moved along through the night, through the edge of the Pittsburgh steel yards. Outside he fancied he could hear the rattle of machinery in the yards, the shouts of the men at their work. Making steel was a twenty-four hour proposition.

Then they were clear of the first set of yards. The car made another switch, and Krenner's heart beat faster. A white sign along the side said, "Private Property. Keep off. Markson Foundries Line." Soon now they would come to a crunching halt. Men would be there, but his gun was intact. No matter how many men he met, he had to get to Markson.

The car shuddered a little, but the acceleration continued. They were rising high in the air now, above the foundries. He looked down, and could see the mighty furnaces thrusting their slim necks to the sky.

A bolt of fear went through him. How far did the automatic system go? Automatic loading of coal from the fields, automatic switching onto the Rolling Roads. Automatic transfer of cars onto a private line which led the cars to the foundries. Where did the automatic handling stop? Where did the *men* come into it? Twenty-seven-year-old concepts slid through his mind, of how freight was carried, of how machines were tended, of how steel was made. In a world of rapidly changing technology, twenty-seven years can bring changes, in every walk of life, in every form of production—

Even steel—

A voice from within him screamed, "Get off, Krenner, get off! This is a one way road—" He climbed quickly to the top of the car, to find a place to jump, and turned back, suddenly sick with fear.

The car was going too fast.

The first car had moved with its load to a high point on the elevated road. A thundering crash came to Krenner's ears as its bottom opened to dislodge its contents. Without stopping. Without men. Automatically. From below he could hear a rushing, roaring sound, and the air was suddenly warmer than before—

The next car followed the first. And the next. Krenner scrambled to the top of the car in rising horror as the car ahead moved serenely, jerked suddenly, and jolted loose its load with a crash of coal against steel. Twenty tons of coal hurtled down a chute into roaring redness—

Twenty-seven years had changed things. He hadn't heard men, for there were no men. No men to tend the fires. Glowing, white-hot furnaces, Markson's furnaces, which were fed on a regular, unerring, merciless consignment belt, running directly from the Roads. Efficient, economical, completely automatic.

Krenner's car gave a jolt that threw his head against the side and shook him down onto the coal load like a bag of potatoes. He clawed desperately for a grip on the side, clawed and missed. The bottom of the car opened, and the load fell through with a roar, and the roar drowned his feeble scream as Krenner fell with the coal.

The last thing he saw below, rushing up, was the glowing, blistering, white-hot maw of the blast furnace.

www.ingramcontent.com/pod-product-compliance
Lightning Source LLC
Chambersburg PA
CBHW030416310726
48979CB00002B/444

* 9 7 9 8 8 8 0 9 0 3 3 9 9 *